DreamWorks

Spirit

HOW TO DRAW

By Kristen Murray • Illustrations by Fabio Laguna

LITTLE, BROWN AND COMPANY
New York • Eoston

SADDLE UP AND GRAB YOUR PENCIL
to draw your best PALs in Miradero!

In this guide, you'll go step-by-step from rough sketches to detailed, finished drawings. Before you hit the frontier, here are a few handy tips and techniques to get you started on your adventure!

HUMAN EYES Front View

Eyes are important for capturing your character's emotion, but they can be tricky to get right. Practice drawing them from different angles until you are comfortable with their shape.

STEP 1

Sketch two circles and add diameter lines. Since the pupils are looking directly at us, these lines will be straight and flat. There is typically one eye's distance between the eyes on a human head.

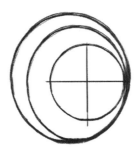 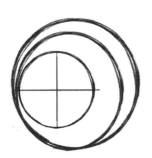

STEP 2

Draw two larger circles around each pupil. These will help outline the shape of the eye and eyelashes.

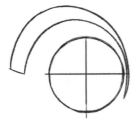 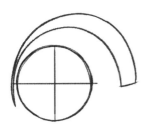

STEP 3

Use these guidelines to sketch the shape of the eyelash lines. Notice how the inner part of the line curves down past the horizontal diameter line.

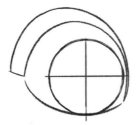 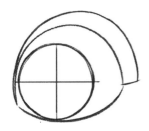

STEP 4

Sketch the position of the lower eyelid. It should meet the base of the pupils. Take care to curve your line upward at the outer edges to ensure the eyes are wide and bright.

HUMAN EYES Front View

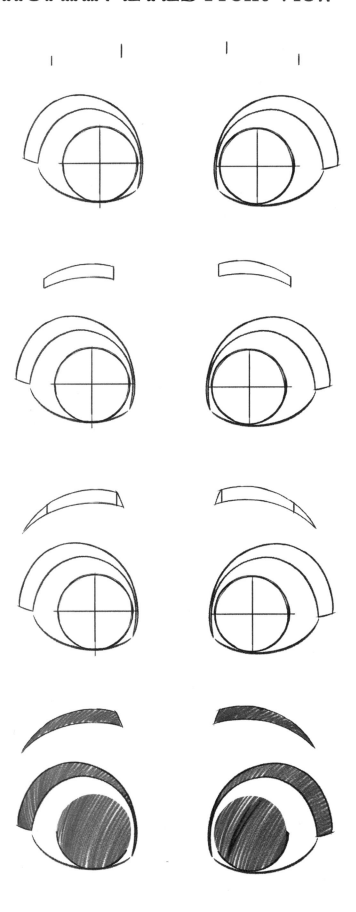

STEP 5
Very lightly sketch short marks above the eye. These will form the eyebrows. The lines near the center of the forehead are slightly higher and longer than those closer to the ears.

STEP 6
Connect your marks with curved lines to form the eyebrows.

STEP 7
Add shape to the eyebrows by drawing small triangles by the inner lines and curving the outer lines to a thin point.

STEP 8
Finish by shading the pupils, eyelashes, and eyebrows with thick black lines.

HORSE EYES Side View

STEP 1
Begin with a small oval shape. Lightly sketch diameter lines through its center.

STEP 2
Draw two curved lines, extending from the top of your oval. They should meet at a point just below the horizontal guideline in your pupil.

STEP 3
Connect the tips of the eyelash lines to the base of your oval.

STEP 4
Sketch two vertical lines, slightly staggered. While the lower mark should align with the tapered point of your lash line, the higher mark should extend farther out, protruding with the forehead.

STEP 5
Use lightly curved lines to join these marks together, extending downward to form a point.

STEP 6
Shade the eyebrows, lash lines, and pupils with heavy strokes.

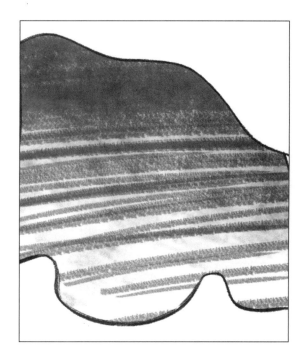

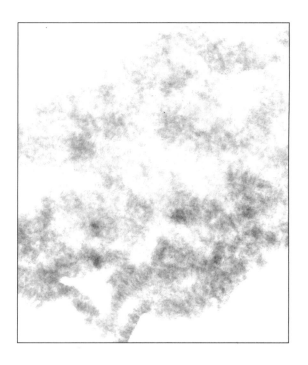

SHADING & TEXTURE

A little bit of shading can turn a flat 2D image into a dynamic 3D illustration. By creating the illusion of form and light with simple shading techniques, you can give clothing the appearance of texture, add depth to your drawings, and make your characters come to life on the page!

Have fun experimenting with different shading methods. Use a smooth back-and-forth motion over an area to create an even tone. Instead of moving in a stiff side-to-side direction, try varying the point where the pencil changes direction to craft interesting textures.

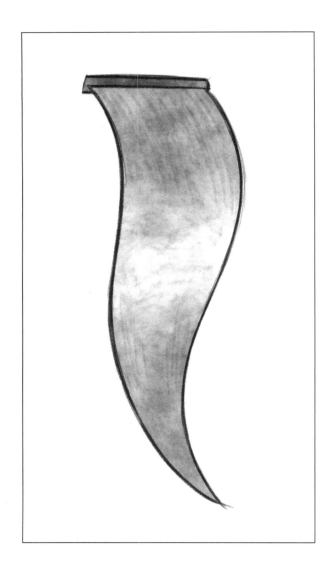

GRADIENTS

Using heavier pressure with the side of your pencil will create dark lines while soft pressure will create light lines. To create realistic shading, gradually transition between both light and heavy strokes. This technique is known as *gradating*.

Hatching is a great technique for shading. Use light, loose lines for a softer effect. Leave more space between your lines when hatching to reflect lighter values. Thick strokes placed tightly together create a smoother shade.

Gradating can give your shading a realistic look. Begin with tight, dark areas where shadows fall and gradually ease the pressure on your pencil as it moves into lighter areas.

Applying heavy pressure to your pencil creates dark lines. The darkest areas will often be where shadows fall on an object. Always consider your light source when shading. Cast shadows will reveal the direction of the light source.

HAIR

Light hatching will add texture to the underside of hair. Each strand of hair moves in a different direction, so don't worry about making these lines too neat or keeping even space between them.

Using small, circular motions rather than straight lines can add texture. Try blending for a smoother transition between light and dark areas by using a blending stick, a tissue, or even your finger.

Combine both techniques to give hair depth. Begin with circular shading to ensure that you don't lose your hatching lines if you choose to blend.

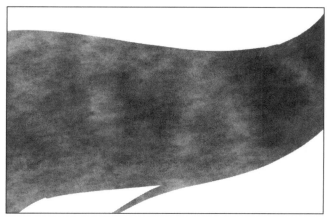

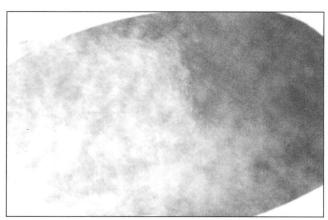

TONES

You will need to use different tones when shading your drawing. Soft B pencils are best for shading as they produce dull, dark lines that are easy to blend. Don't worry if you don't have a range of pencils—standard HB pencils are just as great!

Keep your lines loose with a little bit of space between them when creating light tones. White highlights add eye-catching detail by revealing the areas where the light source reflects most vividly off the object's surface. These can be added later with an eraser.

Mid-tones tend to reflect the actual color of an object in a black-and-white drawing. Begin with light pressure and gradually add layers of shading to reach your desired tone.

Applying heavy pressure to your pencil will create dark, dense areas of shading. Keep your lines close together when shading darkly for a harder look.

Keep consistent pressure on your pencil when shading to achieve smooth strokes. When transitioning between light and dark areas, gradually vary the pressure applied to your pencil to create a gradient effect instead of an abrupt change.

Combining all your shading techniques will help you add shape to your drawings.

CLOTHING

Fabric surfaces absorb light, meaning there should be a smooth transition between highlights and shadows when shading material. Using light lines when shading clothes will create a soft appearance. Consider the material, too: Thinner materials will have more creases, while thicker material will have bigger folds.

Break up white areas with heavy lines to reveal where shadows fall. This stark difference between dark and bright areas is known as *high-contrast shading*. Adding a few spread-out lines under dense areas of shading creates an area of transition as the shadow fades.

DETAIL & PATTERNS

Adding a pattern can completely change an outfit and add personality to your drawing.

Try experimenting with different designs! Patterns can look different depending on the material they are on—a straight line might not appear straight if it's on the curve of a swishing skirt or the crease in a sleeve! These lines should follow the curve and flow of the material to help create a 3D effect.

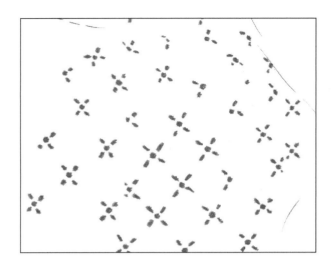

1. A series of dots and dashes create this simple but effective pattern. Surround each dot with four small dashes. Try to keep your dots evenly spaced.

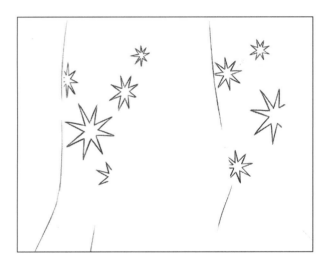

2. Drawing neat eight-point stars can take some practice. Using a ruler, lightly sketch your star's framework by drawing one horizontal line, one vertical line, and two diagonal lines. The center point of all these lines should overlap. The tip of each line will be a point on your star!

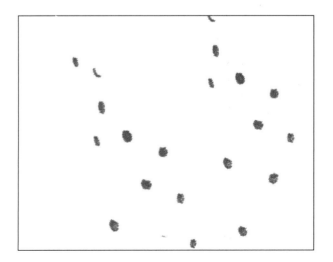

3. Instead of drawing precise round circles and filling them in with dark shading to create stand-out polka dots, try moving the edge of your pencil back and forth in tiny motions to build interesting circular shapes.

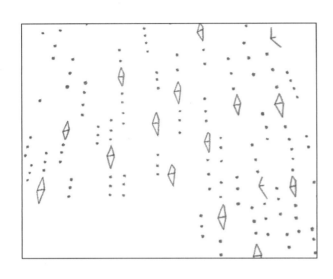

4. Patterns can be broken down into simple shapes to make them less complicated. Diamonds and dots form this pattern. Leave lots of white space to make it stand out!

5. S-curve lines are the prominent shape in this pattern. Draw large S shapes, emphasizing the curl at each end. Add an additional curled line at the wide bend in the lower part of the S shape. Highlight each curl with a series of dashes. Have fun experimenting with different types of lines when creating patterns.

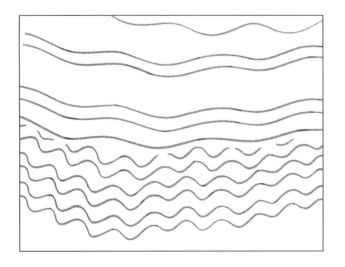

6. Adapting your pattern to follow the flow of the material will create a realistic effect. Notice how the space between the vertical lines changes depending on the position of the curve. The flatter the line, the bigger the space.

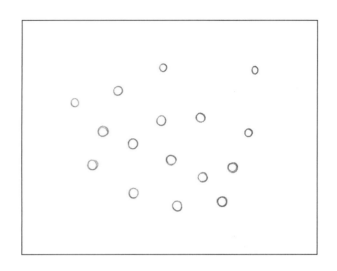

7. Small, precise circles create a simple but attractive pattern. Although it doesn't need to be perfect, try to keep even space between each circle to avoid an overcrowded look.

8. Flowers add lovely detail to an outfit, but they don't have to be complicated to draw. Begin by drawing a firm circle and shading it darkly. Add petals by drawing a series of curved lines.

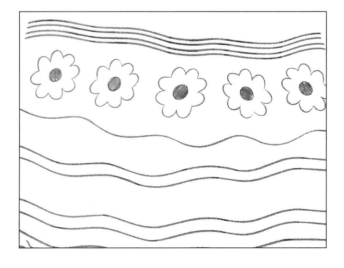

9. Curved lines add a dynamic pattern while wavy lines create a softer appearance.

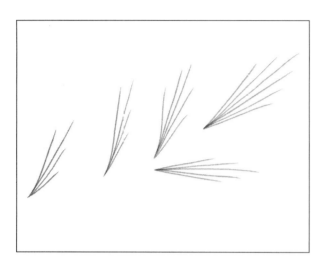

10. Just a few random, straight lines can create texture in a drawing.

11. Grouping lines of different length together can give your drawing a dynamic look. Try to follow the shape of the material. For example, lines will curve with the soft folds in petals, but should be sharp and straight when the object is rigid.

HOW TO DRAW:
LUCKY'S
EVERYDAY OUTFIT

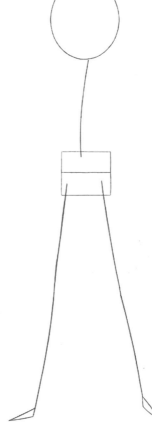

1. Start by establishing the lines of action. To draw Lucky in her confident pose, sketch a large circle for her head and lines for her spine and legs.

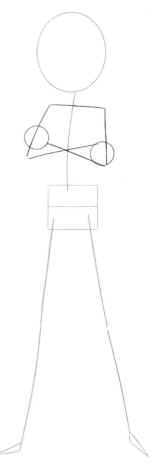

2. Using thin lines, finish Lucky's framework. Keep your pencil marks light so they are easy to erase.

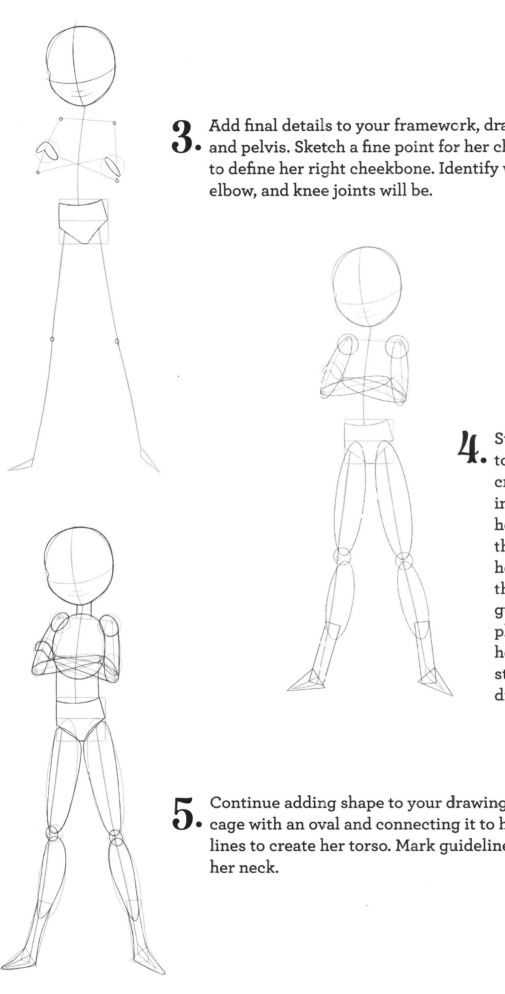

3. Add final details to your framework, drawing Lucky's hands and pelvis. Sketch a fine point for her chin and a slight indent to define her right cheekbone. Identify where her shoulder, elbow, and knee joints will be.

4. Start adding shape to Lucky's limbs. Her crossed-arm pose can be intimidating to draw. Keep her shoulders low rather than hunched up to reflect her relaxed stance. From there, the rest of your guides should fall into place. Taking time to get her position right at this stage will make your final drawing stand out.

5. Continue adding shape to your drawing, outlining Lucky's rib cage with an oval and connecting it to her pelvis with two short lines to create her torso. Mark guidelines on her face and draw her neck.

6. Draw Lucky's facial features. The bottoms of her large eyes touch the horizontal guideline to reflect the tilt in her head, while the bridge of her nose follows the vertical line. Sketch the shape of her hair. It should be long with curled tips to reflect her free-spirited personality!

7. It's time to start drawing detail! Sketch a sash around Lucky's waist and add shape to her shirt and boots.

8. Erase your guidelines and add finer detail to your drawing. Use light lines to create sections in her hair and bold lines to define Lucky's shape and fill in her large eyes, lashes, and brows. Draw a floral design on her shirt and sketch the design on her flame-covered riding boots.

9. Erase any rough linework. Add finishing touches to your drawing. Use hatching to add depth to her hair. Draw a series of triangles around the pattern on Lucky's shirt, taking care not to press too hard, to create contrast in the design.

10. Finish by shading your drawing. Leave thin highlights in the center of each leg to create the illusion of light reflecting off her pants. Add value to Lucky's treasured boots, but keep the flame bright white to make the design pop. All right! You're ready for adventure!

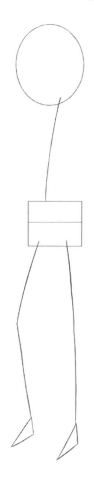

1. Start by establishing the lines of action. Sketch an oval for Pru's head and lines for her spine and legs.

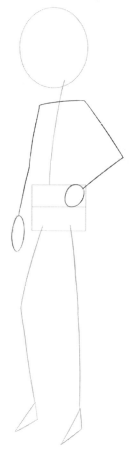

2. Continue building her framework. Keep Pru's posture in mind. Her body is angled confidently, so the parts of her body closest to the viewer's eyeline will appear bigger than those tilted farther away.

3. Sketch the shape of Pru's head, paying attention to the angle of her face. The lines will curve in around her cheekbone and jawline. Outline her pelvis, carefully copying the reference picture to get the angle right.

4. When you're happy with your framework, start adding shape to Pru's limbs. Her stance impacts positioning here. Notice that the guidelines don't run down the center of her right leg, since it's being viewed from the side.

5. Continue fleshing out your outline. Draw her neck. Sketch an oval for Pru's rib cage, using short lines to connect it to her pelvis. Consider the shape of these lines to create the curve in her back.

6. Draw Pru's facial features. Although her head is tilted, she is looking directly at the viewer. The right eye should appear more circular in shape than the left at this angle. The edge of each pupil line should fall in the middle of each eye, regardless of shape. Outline her curly hair. Don't forget her ribbon!

7. Outline Pru's outfit. Her overalls follow her body shape, but their cuffs are wide. Try drawing two small squares, then soften their edges. Pencil gentle curves in the fold in the elbow of her shirt, giving it a more fluid look than the stiff denim folds of her overalls.

8. Let's add some detail! Remember—everything can be broken down into basic shapes. A square and triangle with softened points create pockets, while rectangles connect to a circle to create the clasp for her overalls. Finally, add curved lines to the body of her hair to create texture. Hair tends to fall in sections, so grouping your lines together will help create a realistic look.

9. Firm up your outline and erase any remaining guidelines. Fill in her eyebrows, eyelashes, and pupils with dark shading.

10. It's time to shade your drawing. Adding darker value to her overalls will create a heavy denim effect, while leaving her shirt white makes the material appear softer. Gradually build layers of shading until you get the tone just right—adding value is easier than erasing dark lines!

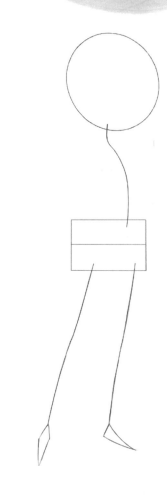

1. Start by establishing the lines of action. Sketch an oval for Abigail's head and a line with a slight curve for her spine. Add two stacked rectangles for her pelvis and lines for her legs and feet.

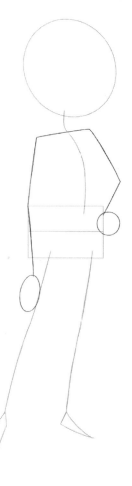

2. Complete her framework, adding lines for her shoulders and arms. Abigail is standing at an angle, so the lines forming her left arm and leg will be slightly shorter than those on her right side. This will help trick the eye and make it appear that her body is tilted. This art trick is called *foreshortening*.

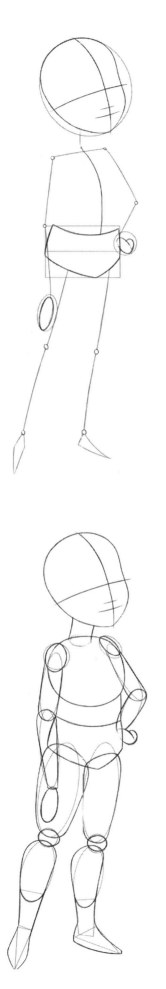

3. Mark the placement of her joints and sketch the shape of her pelvis. Outline her head, indenting the lines slightly around her cheekbones. Carefully mark guidelines on her face, following the curve of her skull.

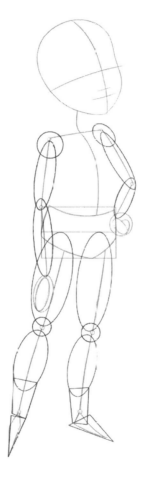

4. Begin adding shape to Abigail's body. Be careful with the positioning of your knee joints here. They will help create the dips in the back of Abigail's knees in the final drawing.

5. Draw a circle for her rib cage and two short lines to form her neck. Her chin should look as if it is turned slightly upward.

6. Following your guides, add Abigail's facial features and ear. The earlobe will sit in line with the guideline for her nose: approximately halfway up her face from her chin. Sketch in the outline of her hair and hair tie.

7. It's time to draw Abigail's outfit! Aside from her billowing sleeves, her shirt, jeans, and boots fit her comfortably and closely follow the outline of her body. Draw a belt and start forming the shape of her boots.

8. Now that Abigail is dressed, it's time to define your outline and erase any remaining guidelines. Use thick black lines to shade her pupils, eyelashes, and eyebrows.

9. Patterns can completely change an outfit! Create the design on Abigail's shirt by surrounding a small circle with four short lines, evenly spacing out each embellishment.

10. Finish by shading your drawing. Experiment with different shading methods to create different textures on clothing. Contrast dark shading on her boots with bright, white highlights on the stars to create a finishing sparkle!

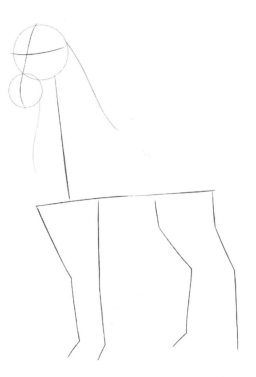

1. Start by establishing the lines of action. Sketch Spirit's framework by drawing two circles, overlapping slightly. This will create his head. Draw a long neckline with a slight bend, that connects to the larger circle, followed by a shorter, curved line connecting to the smaller circle to create his tall stance.

2. Continue building Spirit's framework. Connect the circles to the base of his body with a long vertical line. Add guidelines to the circles, arching the vertical line at his muzzle.

3. With your framework in place, start adding shape to Spirit's body. Horses can be intimidating to draw but can be broken down into basic shapes: two large circles for his body; a large trapezoid for his neck; and ovals, circles, and trapezoids for his legs and hooves.

4. Draw an outline around the two circles to form Spirit's body, creating a shape like a peanut! Sketch Spirit's hooves. Notice how their shape changes slightly depending on the angle of his feet.

5. Working down from his jawline, continue defining Spirit's outline. Add shape to his legs. The outline closely follows the guidelines around his hocks and fetlocks. Lightly sketch his ears.

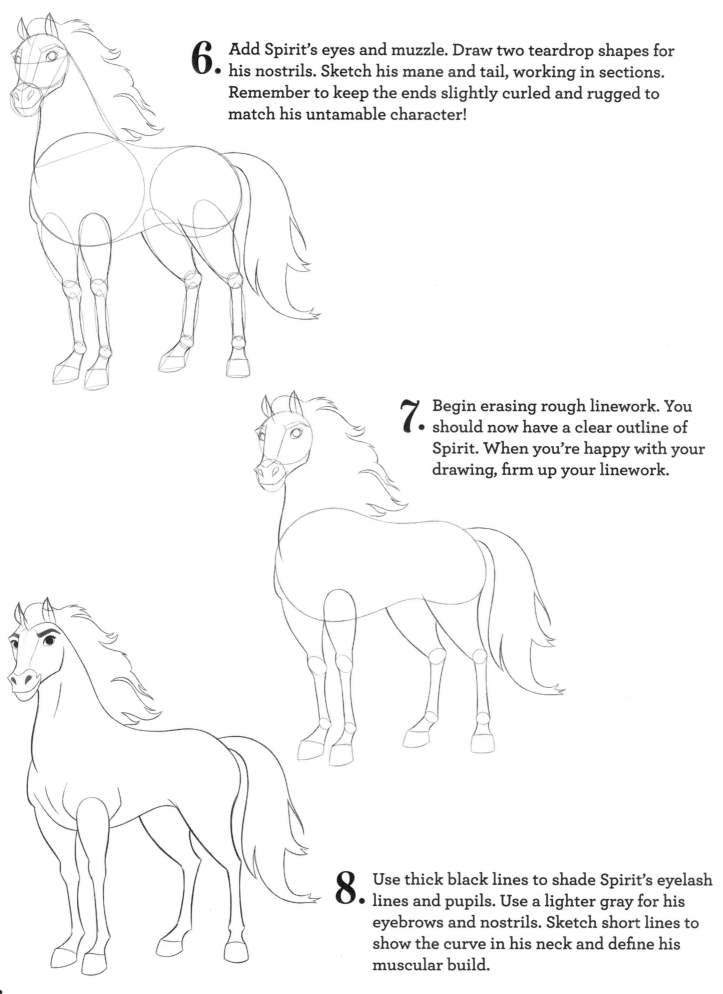

6. Add Spirit's eyes and muzzle. Draw two teardrop shapes for his nostrils. Sketch his mane and tail, working in sections. Remember to keep the ends slightly curled and rugged to match his untamable character!

7. Begin erasing rough linework. You should now have a clear outline of Spirit. When you're happy with your drawing, firm up your linework.

8. Use thick black lines to shade Spirit's eyelash lines and pupils. Use a lighter gray for his eyebrows and nostrils. Sketch short lines to show the curve in his neck and define his muscular build.

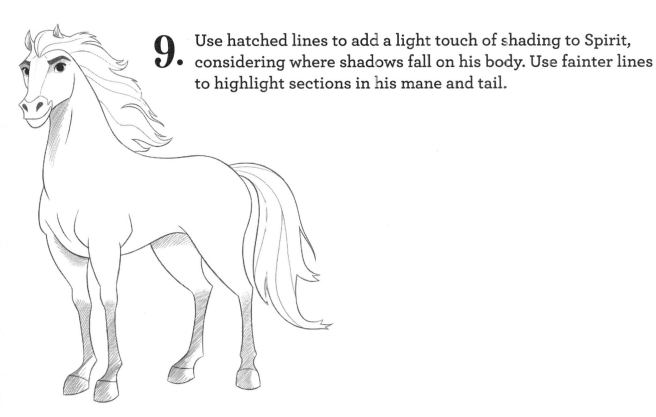

9. Use hatched lines to add a light touch of shading to Spirit, considering where shadows fall on his body. Use fainter lines to highlight sections in his mane and tail.

10. Finish by carefully blending your hatched lines to create softer tones. Be careful not to smudge his clean coat. Shade his mane and tail. You're ready to ride free!

HOW TO DRAW:
CHICA LINDA STANDING

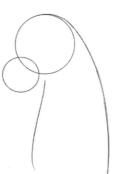

1. To draw the most beautiful horse in Miradero, establish the lines of action. Sketch two circles, overlapping them slightly. Draw a long, curved line extending down from the larger circle and a shorter line from the smaller circle.

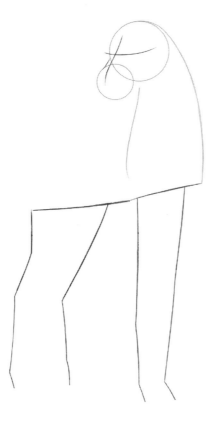

2. Continue building Chica Linda's framework, using long lines to sketch her body and legs, capturing her tall, proud pose. Mark guidelines on her face, curving across her muzzle.

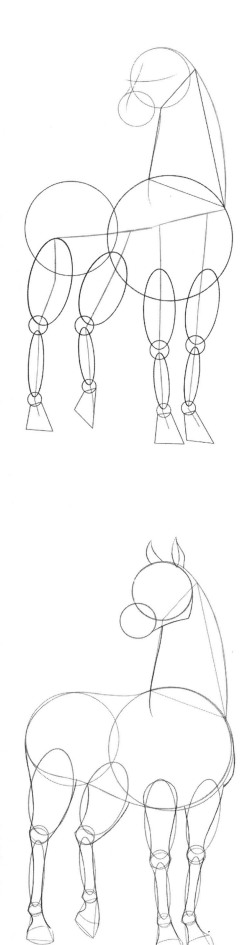

3. Add shape to Chica Linda's outline. Break each body part down into basic shapes: large circles for her body, a large trapezoid for her neck and smaller ones for her feet, and ovals and circles for her legs.

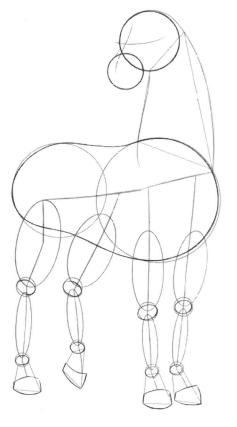

4. Connect the two circles to create the main outline of her body. Define the shape of her hooves. These can be tricky to get right, but each hoof is unique! Practice drawing hooves at different angles to get comfortable with their form.

5. Sketch her ears and jawline, then draw a curved line for her neck. Add shape to her muscular legs, with the lines tapering in closely around her joints. Carefully copy the shape of the rear leg, which is slightly raised.

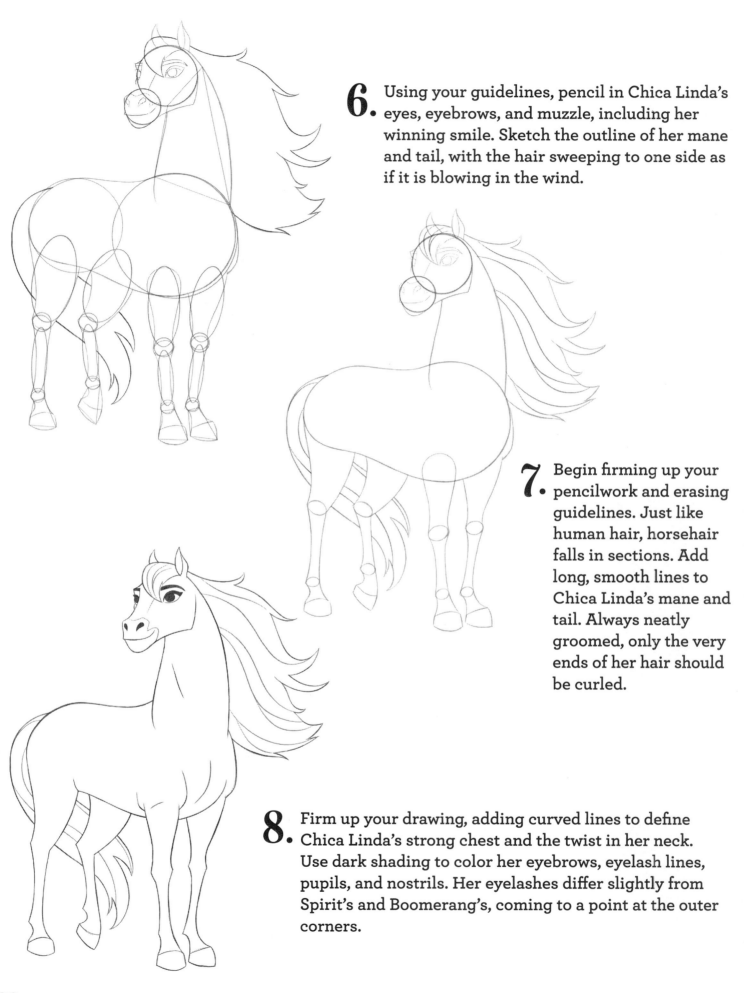

6. Using your guidelines, pencil in Chica Linda's eyes, eyebrows, and muzzle, including her winning smile. Sketch the outline of her mane and tail, with the hair sweeping to one side as if it is blowing in the wind.

7. Begin firming up your pencilwork and erasing guidelines. Just like human hair, horsehair falls in sections. Add long, smooth lines to Chica Linda's mane and tail. Always neatly groomed, only the very ends of her hair should be curled.

8. Firm up your drawing, adding curved lines to define Chica Linda's strong chest and the twist in her neck. Use dark shading to color her eyebrows, eyelash lines, pupils, and nostrils. Her eyelashes differ slightly from Spirit's and Boomerang's, coming to a point at the outer corners.

9. Shade your drawing, carefully considering where light hits her body and where shadows fall. Use soft motions with your pencil to gradually add value to the darkest areas. Your drawing is worthy of a blue ribbon!

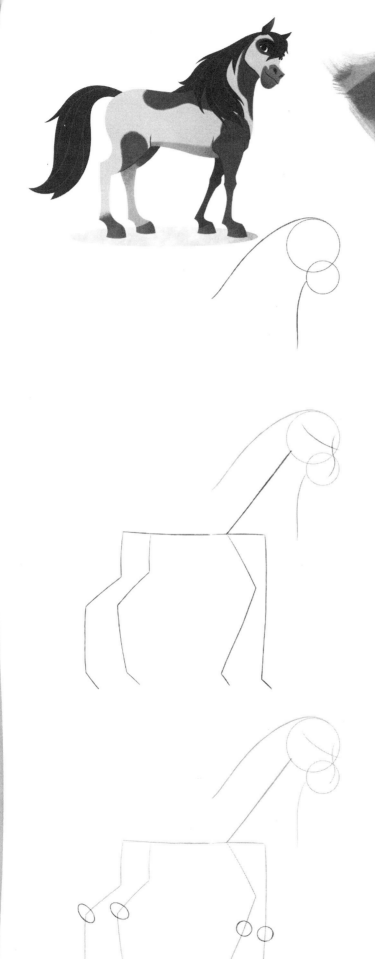

1. Start by establishing the lines of action. Using circles to build an outline can make drawing horses easier. Sketch two circles, the smaller one slightly overlapping the larger one. Draw a long line extending down from the top of the larger circle, with a shorter line coming from the smaller circle.

2. Use straight lines to build Boomerang's framework. Add guidelines to his face, taking care to curve them around his muzzle. Copy the shape from the reference picture to help place his features symmetrically.

3. Carefully mark Boomerang's joints, using circles for his front knees and fetlocks (ankles), and ovals for his hocks (back knees) and rear fetlocks. Use curved lines to add the shape of his hooves.

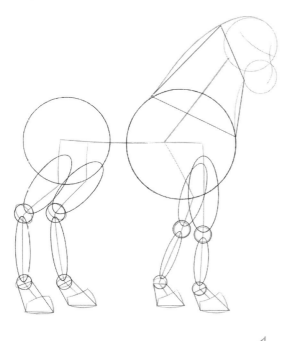

4. Continue building Boomerang's shape. Sketch two large circles, one slightly larger than the other. Trapezoids create his neck and feet, while cylinders and circles form his legs.

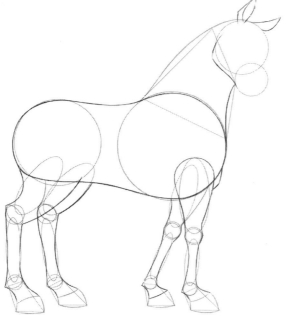

5. Sketch Boomerang's pointy ears, then start adding form to his body. His jaw creates a large L shape. Curl his neckline down to meet his chest, and draw lines around the two large circles to clearly outline his body. Begin defining the shape of his legs.

6. Draw Boomerang's friendly expression. As his head is cocked to the side, follow your guidelines carefully to place his features. Sketch the shape of his long, flowing mane and tail.

7. Add sections of hair to Boomerang's mane and tail, using light, wavy lines to show how the hair falls around his body. Outline the distinctive patches on his coat and around his eye.

8. Firm up your outline and erase any remaining rough pencilwork. It's time to start adding detail! Shade Boomerang's eyebrows, eyelash lines, pupils, and nostrils.

9. Finish by adding value to your drawing. Boomerang is a pinto gelding, meaning his coat is largely white with colored patches, so use your eraser to clean up any smudges and keep his coat clean and bright! Use short, soft strokes with your pencil when shading the dark patches to help show the direction in which the finer horsehair lies.

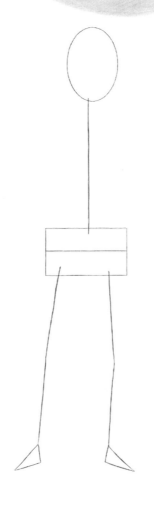

1. Start by establishing the lines of action. Draw your framework. Jim is tall and slim, so keep your oval thin and sketch long vertical lines for his spine and legs.

2. Continue sketching your framework. Jim's body is facing straight forward in this pose, so these lines will be even. Remember, nobody is perfectly symmetrical, so don't worry too much about precision!

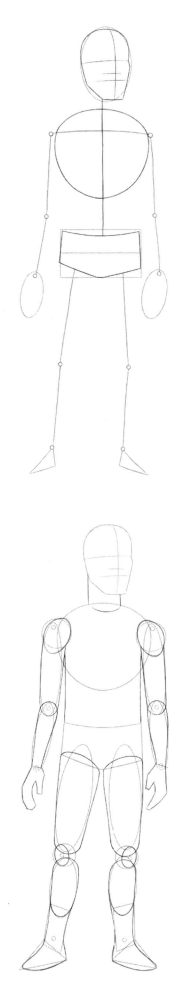

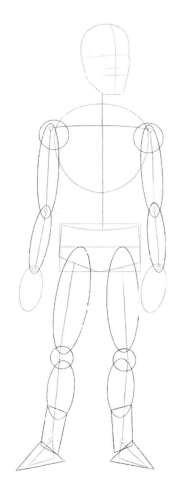

3. Add shape to Jim's head, squaring his jawline. Sketch guidelines on his face and mark the position of your figure's joints with small circles. Draw a wide oval for Jim's rib cage and sketch his pelvis.

4. It's time to start fleshing out the drawing. To reflect Jim's slim build, keep the outline close to the framework.

5. Continue adding shape to Jim's body. Round off the shoulders to help create a relaxed stance. Define the shape of his legs to fit his straight-legged pants and round the toes of his boots.

6. Outline Jim's facial features. His lips are thin, so use two simple lines to create his smile. Draw his hair, making sure it doesn't sit flat on his head. Lightly sketch his vest and shirt.

7. Sketch the outline of Jim's hat. This can be broken into simple shapes. Begin with a large oval for the brim and a smaller circle to outline the crown. To create the brim's curve, draw a long S shape through the oval. An arched line in the center of the circle outlines the hat's ribbon.

8. Start firming up your pencilwork, adding detail to Jim's clothing. Use faint lines to depict creases on his shirt. Sketch a soft diagonal line on his neck, creating the illusion his head is slightly turned.

9. Pencil in the outline of his hat and erase any remaining rough lines. Color in Jim's pupils and eyebrows with firm strokes.

10. Add value to your drawing, gradually increasing pressure in darker areas. Shade Jim's chin to create stubble. Use a light stippling effect with a soft pencil to give it a rough texture.

HOW TO DRAW:
AUNT CORA

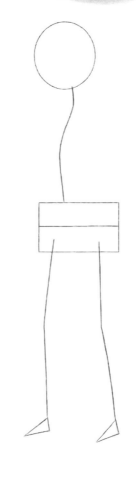

1. Start by establishing the lines of action. Sketch a circle for Aunt Cora's head and a gently curved line for her spine. Add two stacked rectangles and lines for her legs and feet.

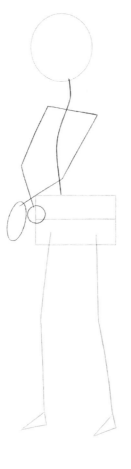

2. Sketch arms as you finish your framework. Aunt Cora's posture is tall and proper, so take care to get her stance just right at this early stage.

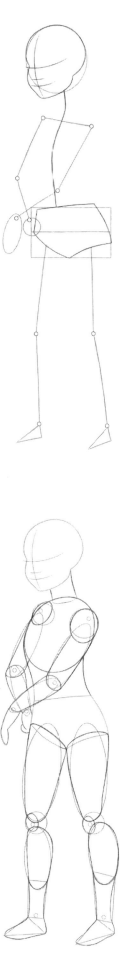

3. Add shape to her head, curving in slightly around her cheekbone and keeping her jawline soft. Considering Aunt Cora's angle, carefully pencil in guidelines for her facial features.

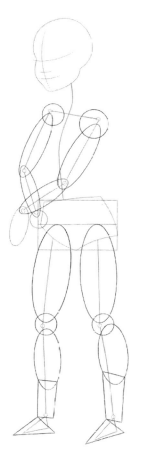

4. Begin fleshing out your framework. Take care when crossing her arms. Though her right wrist is covered, it is useful to sketch it in place at this stage to ensure your proportions are correct.

5. Continue adding shape to Aunt Cora's outline. Sketch an oval to form her rib cage and arched lines to form her torso. Start defining her hands.

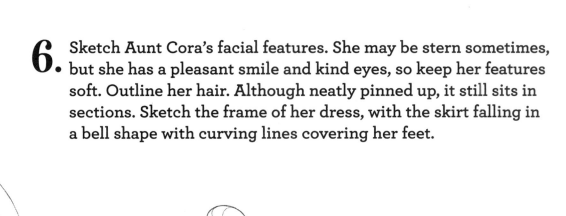

6. Sketch Aunt Cora's facial features. She may be stern sometimes, but she has a pleasant smile and kind eyes, so keep her features soft. Outline her hair. Although neatly pinned up, it still sits in sections. Sketch the frame of her dress, with the skirt falling in a bell shape with curving lines covering her feet.

7. Create texture on Cora's skirt by drawing a series of thin vertical lines, following the flow of the material. Keep these lines soft rather than rigid. Add a pattern to her top. It looks complicated but can be created by using small triangles.

8. Firm up your outline and erase any remaining guidelines. Color her pupils, eyelashes, and eyebrows with heavy lines.

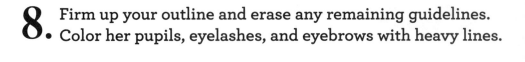

9. Use circular motions to shade your drawing, gradually building value in the darker areas. Hair reflects light and has a variety of tones, so play with highlights and dark value in her hair to make it look realistic.

1. Start by establishing the lines of action. Draw an oval for Al's head. His head is angled toward the viewer, so keep your oval slim. Draw a diagonal line to form the upper part of his spine, two stacked rectangles for his pelvis, lines for his legs, and triangles for his feet.

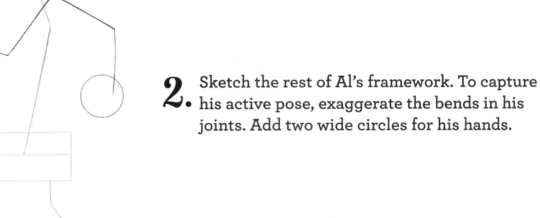

2. Sketch the rest of Al's framework. To capture his active pose, exaggerate the bends in his joints. Add two wide circles for his hands.

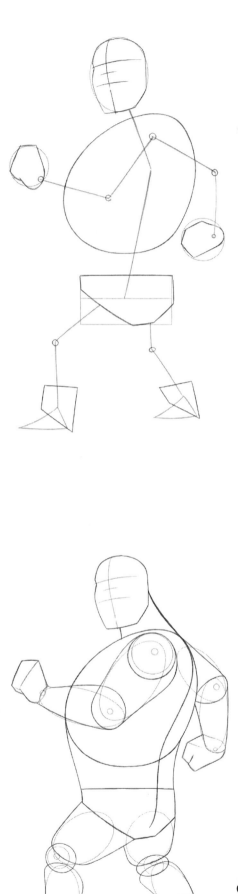

3. Sketch a large egg shape for Al's rib cage. Make it oversize to show off his strength from wrangling wild stallions! Outline his pelvis and hands. Reshape his head, keeping his jaw square. Sketch a trapezoid beside each foot to help shape his boots.

4. Start adding shape to your framework. Al is much larger than the PALs, so use wider ovals and circles when drawing his outline to create his bulky figure.

5. Curve lines down from his rib cage to meet his pelvis. Drawing in his waist slightly will help emphasize his muscular build. Continue adding shape to his hands, considering where his knuckles bend to form a fist.

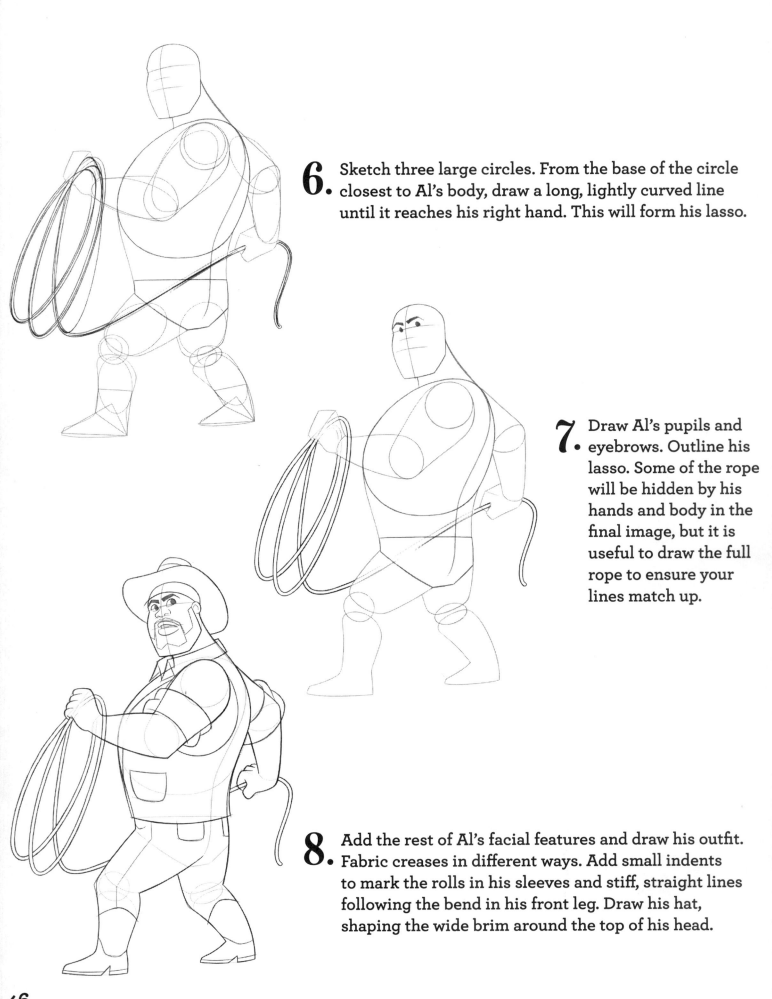

6. Sketch three large circles. From the base of the circle closest to Al's body, draw a long, lightly curved line until it reaches his right hand. This will form his lasso.

7. Draw Al's pupils and eyebrows. Outline his lasso. Some of the rope will be hidden by his hands and body in the final image, but it is useful to draw the full rope to ensure your lines match up.

8. Add the rest of Al's facial features and draw his outfit. Fabric creases in different ways. Add small indents to mark the rolls in his sleeves and stiff, straight lines following the bend in his front leg. Draw his hat, shaping the wide brim around the top of his head.

9. Tidy up your overall outline and erase any remaining guidelines. Notice how the brim of the hat sits low on Al's forehead.

10. Finish by adding value to your drawing. Don't be afraid to use a range of tones when shading to make your character come to life. You're ready to wrangle Spirit and his herd—if you can catch them!

HOW TO DRAW:
SNIPS STONE

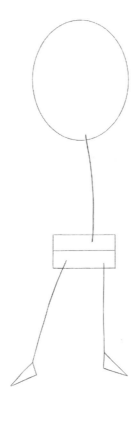

1. Start by establishing the lines of action. Sketch a large oval and lines for Snips Stone's head, spine, and lower body.

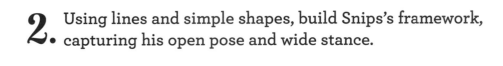

2. Using lines and simple shapes, build Snips's framework, capturing his open pose and wide stance.

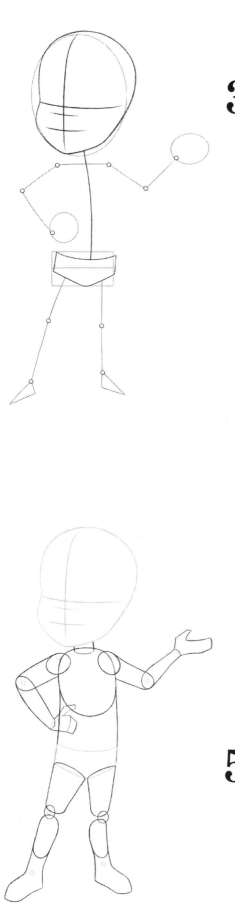

3. Carefully mark all of Snips's joints with small circles. Reshape his jawline and outline his head, which is turned toward the right. Sketch guidelines on his face. Snips is still young, so his eyeline sits slightly below the center of his head. Outline his pelvis.

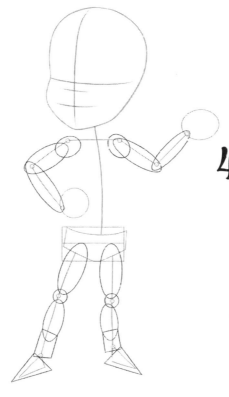

4. With your framework now complete, start adding shape to Snips's body. Take care when creating his outline. Notice how his outstretched pose slightly skews the proportions of the shapes.

5. Sketch an oval for his rib cage and add two lines to form his torso. Begin defining the shape of his hands and boots. You should now have a clear outline of Snips's body.

6. Draw his facial features. As his head is at an angle, his right eye sits closer to the vertical guideline. Small dots create freckles. His hair arches over his head, moving away from the soft tuft around his part. Sketch the outline for his clothes, with his shorts falling just below his knees and his socks pulled up his calves.

7. Firm up your outline and erase any remaining guidelines. To add detail to Snips's outfit, pencil in soft rolls around his socks and sleeves, as well as laces on his shoes. When drawing shoes, it can be helpful to imagine the shape of the foot inside to get proportions right.

8. Use heavy shading to fill in Snips's eyebrows, eyelashes, and pupils. Notice that his eyelashes don't peak at the outer corners like the PALs' lashes.

9. Shade your drawing using short, steady lines for shadowy areas. Use gentle circular motions for his hair, shirt, and shoes to add texture. Transition gradually between light and heavy pressure when shading his sweater to create a realistic look.

HOW TO DRAW: MILAGRO PRESCOTT

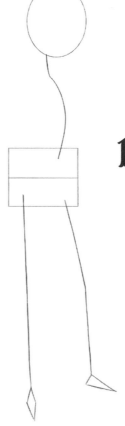

1. Start by establishing the lines of action. Sketch an oval for Lucky's mom's head and thin lines to begin her framework.

2. Continue building the framework. Milagro's body is turned to one side, so use foreshortening to capture her stance: By adjusting the size of your lines, it's possible to trick the eye and create a 3D effect. Notice how the lines forming her right limbs appear longer than those forming her left limbs. It can be helpful to practice drawing stick figures from different perspectives to get the hang of this technique!

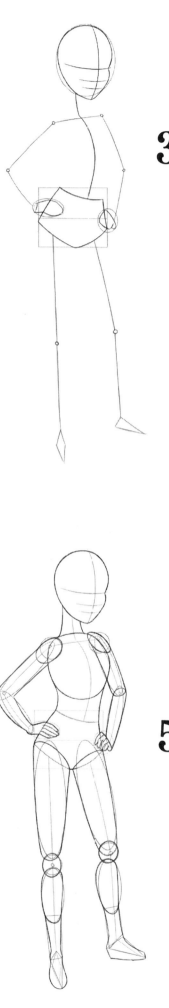

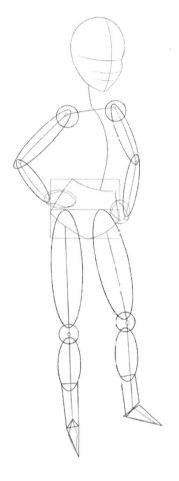

3. Reshape Milagro's face, making her jawline more angular, and mark guidelines for her eyes, nose, and mouth. Draw the outline of her pelvis, carefully copying the reference image to get the angle right.

4. Using your framework, start adding shape to Milagro's body.

5. Draw Milagro's neck and a circle for her rib cage. Define her fingers, noticing how they bend. Use your own hand as a reference to examine how fingers flex and curl.

6. Sketch Milagro's facial features, following your guidelines carefully. Draw her long hair with large curls at the tips. Create the outline of her earring by stacking wide, thin U shapes. Add a heel to her boot.

7. Outline Milagro's dress. Although her skirt is wide, the fabric follows the shape of her body, curving more at the back while gently descending at the front. Draw wide egg shapes to create her puffed sleeves.

8. Firm up your outlines and erase any remaining guidelines. Use thick black shading to fill in Milagro's pupils, eyelashes, and eyebrows. Eyelashes are drawn as a solid mass rather than individual lines and reach a peak at the outside corners.

9. Let's add some detail to Milagro's dress! Draw flowers on her sleeves and skirt. Pencil in small circles to her top and draw a series of wavy lines on her skirt.

10. Sketch curved lines to give Milagro's scarf a textured appearance as it drapes around her waist. A few short vertical lines on her skirt will create folds in the thick fabric. Continue building the pattern on her tiered skirt, adding more wavy lines.

11. Add some light shading to your drawing using the edge of your pencil. Although Milagro has dark hair, avoid using heavy lines when adding value. Experimenting with pressure on your pencil can create a textured look and leaving brighter areas of highlights can help add volume and shape.

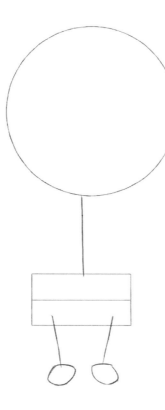

1. Start by establishing the lines of action. Sketch Lucky's frame. Proportions change as characters age. Lucky's head is much larger as a baby, so use a big circle instead of an oval. Use short, straight lines for her legs, two rectangles for her hips, and two little lemon shapes for her feet.

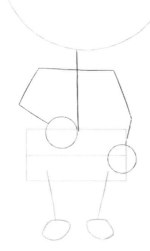

2. Continue building Lucky's framework, sketching short, straight lines for her shoulders and arms, with circles for her hands.

56

3. Add guidelines for Lucky's facial features. As a baby, Lucky's eyes are very large and will sit low on her head. Start firming up the shape of her hands and sketch the outline of her pelvis.

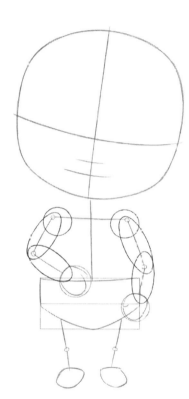

4. Flesh out your framework. To capture her cute limbs, your ovals should be short and wide, sitting far from the frame lines.

5. Continue building Lucky's form. Pencil in an oval for her chest, joining it to her pelvic outline. These lines should curve out at her waist, giving her an adorable figure. Sketch wide ovals around her knee joints.

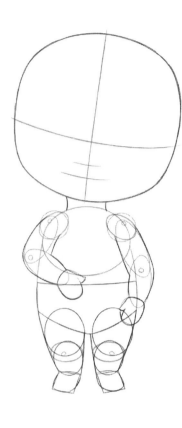

6. Sketch in the shape of her legs. Again, keep your ovals short and wide here, overlapping with the knee joints to ensure her legs have a babyish look.

7. Add detail to Lucky's face, exaggerating the size of her wide eyes. Sketch her hair in sections. Have fun drawing her short, curly hair and don't worry about making lines really neat. Adding loose strands can create a more natural look.

8. Outline Lucky's dress. The hem should sit just below her knees. The material falls around her, so use faint, curved lines to create the outfit's smooth form. Firm up your pencilwork and erase any remaining guidelines.

9. Add decorative detail to Lucky's dress. To draw a simple strawberry, sketch a triangle and round the corners to form its body. Mark small black dots in the center of the shape to create the seeds. Finish by sketching a small crown shape for the stem.

10. It's time to start shading. Add long, thick strokes to Lucky's eyebrows, eyelashes, and eyes. Follow the curve of each shape to create a natural contour effect.

11. Carefully shade Lucky's hair, using circular motions with your pencil to create a soft look. Work line by line to layer harder strokes in the darkest areas. Considering where shadows fall on her dress, add a light touch of shading to her body and outfit.

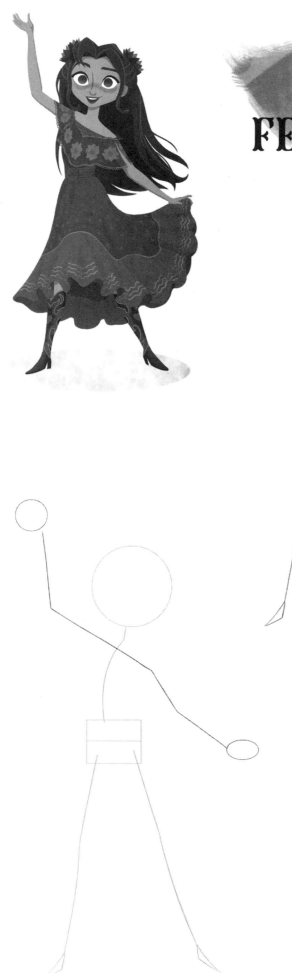

HOW TO DRAW: LUCKY'S FESTIVAL OUTFIT

1. Start by establishing the lines of action. Sketch the framework for Lucky's head and body, taking care to capture the curve in her spine. This will help form her dynamic pose.

2. Continue building your framework, using long lines for her arms.

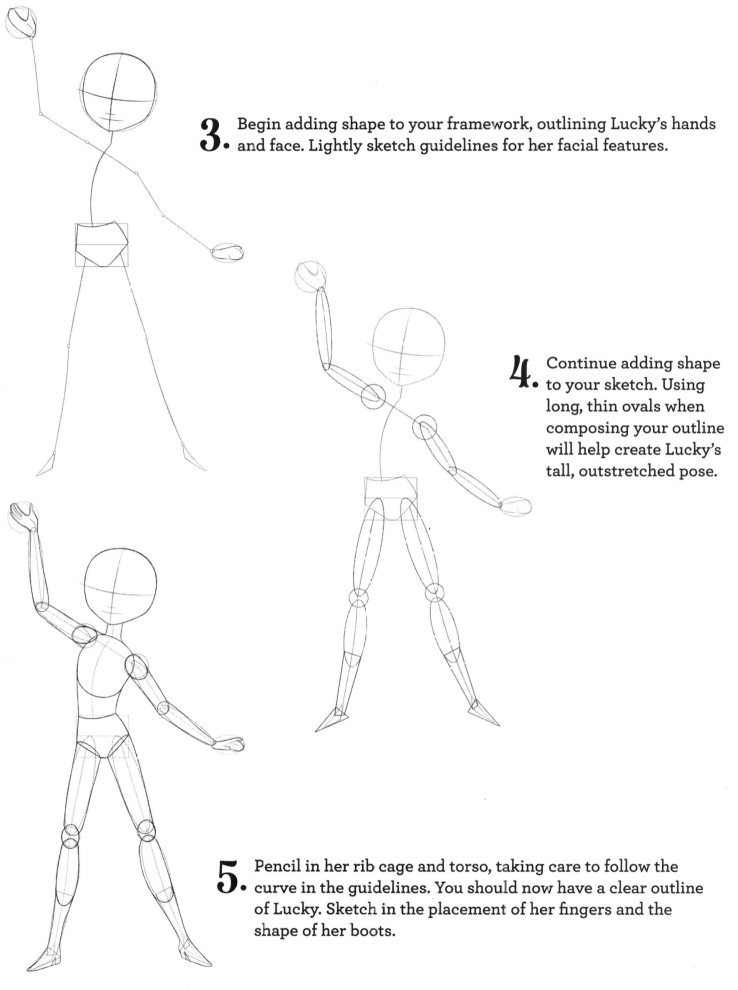

3. Begin adding shape to your framework, outlining Lucky's hands and face. Lightly sketch guidelines for her facial features.

4. Continue adding shape to your sketch. Using long, thin ovals when composing your outline will help create Lucky's tall, outstretched pose.

5. Pencil in her rib cage and torso, taking care to follow the curve in the guidelines. You should now have a clear outline of Lucky. Sketch in the placement of her fingers and the shape of her boots.

6. Draw Lucky's facial features, capturing her happy expression. Outline her hair with long sections sweeping to the left to capture her movement as she dances. Sketch triangles with rounded edges to add the two large flowers to her hair.

7. Outline Lucky's dress. Use random wavy lines to create the dress's shape and keep it from falling flat. Adding folds under the fabric can help create a 3D effect. Notice how the skirt moves away from Lucky's body, curling up into her hand.

8. Firm up your outlines and erase rough linework. Shade Lucky's eyebrows, eyelashes, and pupils. Pencil scalloped lines to decorate the top of her dress, as well as random lines to add texture to her clothing, considering how the fabric falls.

9. Sketch simple flowers on Lucky's top. Draw a series of S-shaped swirls to her skirt. Highlight each curl with short lines to create an attractive pattern.

10. Finish by adding value to your drawing. When shading Lucky's underskirt, use heavy, compact strokes in the darkest areas, easing pressure slightly and relaxing your wrist while you sweep the pencil across the page in back-and-forth motions as you work down.

HOW TO DRAW: PRU'S FESTIVAL OUTFIT

1. Start by establishing the lines of action. Draw Pru's celebratory pose by sketching her head; spine; and long, outstretched legs.

2. Sketch a series of lines to create Pru's full framework. Her shoulders are angled in this pose.

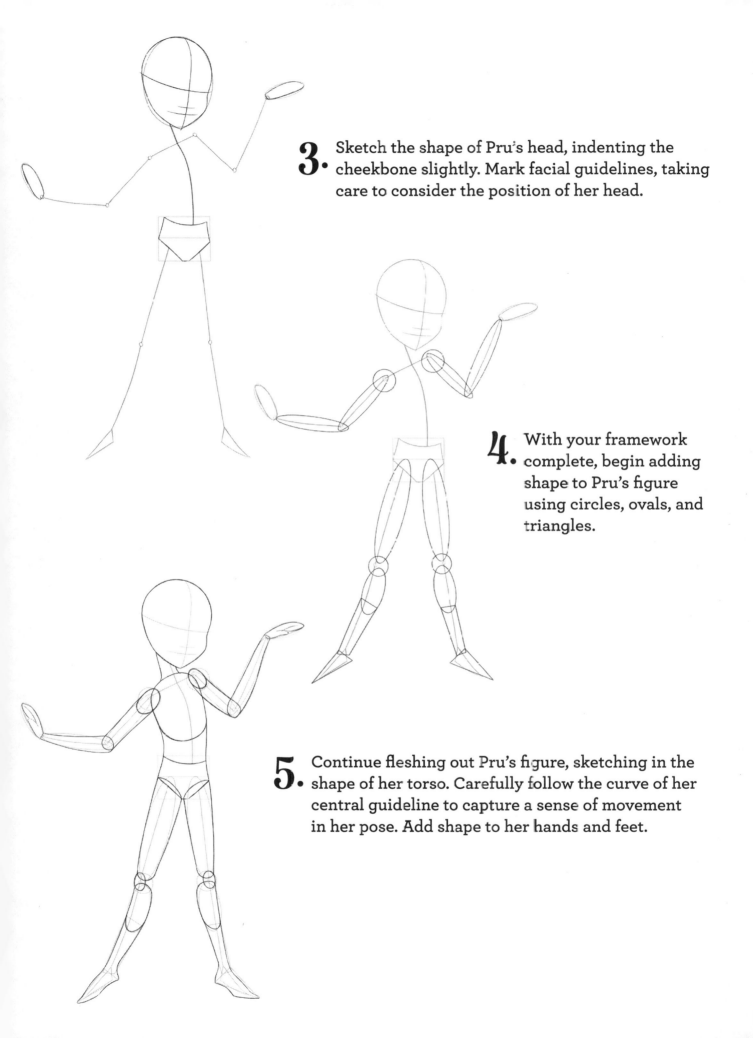

3. Sketch the shape of Pru's head, indenting the cheekbone slightly. Mark facial guidelines, taking care to consider the position of her head.

4. With your framework complete, begin adding shape to Pru's figure using circles, ovals, and triangles.

5. Continue fleshing out Pru's figure, sketching in the shape of her torso. Carefully follow the curve of her central guideline to capture a sense of movement in her pose. Add shape to her hands and feet.

6. Pencil in Pru's facial features. Outline her hair, using soft, curved lines until the strands meet at the tip of her trademark ponytail. Indent the hair slightly where the ribbon ties around it.

7. Draw Pru's dress with the skirt billowing out to give it shape. Use long, curved lines to create a sense of movement in the fabric. Sketch the outline of her boots, with the cuffs extending away from her ankles.

8. Erase any remaining guidelines. Shade Pru's brows, eyelashes, and pupils. It's time to add detail! Decorate Pru's outfit, breaking the patterns down into basic shapes: triangles around the neckline, circles for the belt and shoe buckles, and a wavy line framing her boots. Use simple lines to create folds in her skirt.

9. Use short, curved lines to create shape in Pru's hair, capturing her curls. Continue adding detail to her dress. When drawing the design around the hem of her skirt, carefully follow the twists and flow of the material to create a 3D effect.

10. The decorative design on Pru's dress can be created by drawing a series of diamonds and small black dots. Leave some white areas on her dress to let the pattern shine!

11. Finish by shading your drawing. Use circular motions with the edge of your pencil to keep the shading soft for this drawing. Including faint areas of shading around the creases in Pru's skirt will help create the illusion that she's dancing on the page!

HOW TO DRAW: ABIGAIL'S FESTIVAL OUTFIT

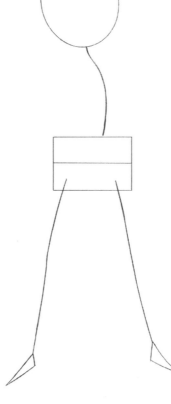

1. Start by establishing the lines of action. Sketch an oval and a short, curved line for Abigail's spine. Then lightly sketch two stacked rectangles for her pelvis, lines for her legs, and outline her feet.

2. Continue building Abigail's framework, lightly sketching lines for her arms and outlining her hands and feet.

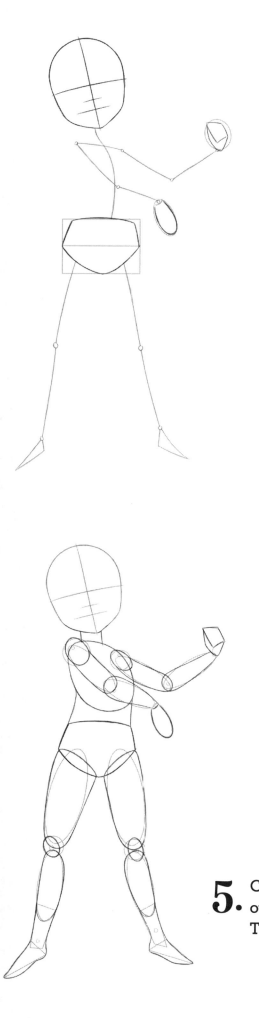

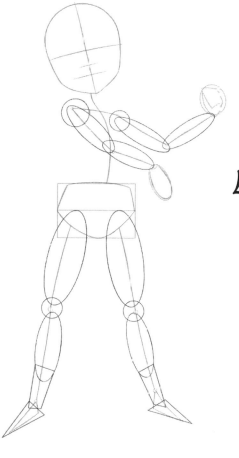

3. Mark the placement of her joints with small circles. Define the shape of the pelvis and sketch guidelines on Abigail's face, adding shape to her jawline.

4. Now that your framework is complete, begin adding shape to your figure: ovals for the arms and legs, circles around the joints, and rectangles and triangles to form her ankles and feet.

5. Continue adding shape to Abigail's body, sketching a large oval to form her rib cage. Start to firm up her overall shape. This will help form her curled fingers in the next step.

6. Use your guidelines to draw Abigail's facial features. Make sure her smile is big and wide! Outline her hair, using sweeping, free-flowing lines to create a sense of movement. Sketch the placement of her hair tie, tucked behind her ears and forming a large knot on the top of her head. Sketch the placement of her fingers.

7. Sketch Abigail's dress and ankle boots. Fabric follows the shape of the body but rarely sits straight. While the top part of Abigail's dress follows her torso closely, the lines of her flowing skirt move away from her body. Draw a small flag in her left hand.

8. Add polka dots to her top and the bottom of her skirt, a scalloped line along her skirt's edge, and small flowers to her belt. Use light pressure when marking their placement, going over them with harder strokes when you're happy with your design.

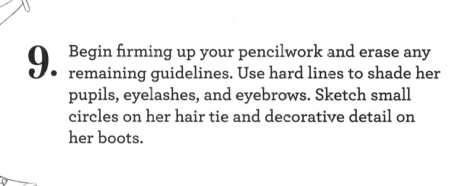

9. Begin firming up your pencilwork and erase any remaining guidelines. Use hard lines to shade her pupils, eyelashes, and eyebrows. Sketch small circles on her hair tie and decorative detail on her boots.

10. With a little bit of shading, Abigail is ready to celebrate! Try using the edge of your pencil to create faint shadows along the folds in her skirt to create a 3D look. Use your eraser to create a bright highlight in the center of her flag to emphasize the curve in the material.

HOW TO DRAW:
SEÑOR CARROTS

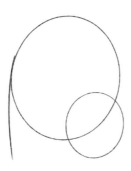

1. Begin drawing Snips's best friend by establishing the lines of action. Sketch a large oval with a smaller oval overlapping it. Sketch a short, arched line, extending down from the larger shape.

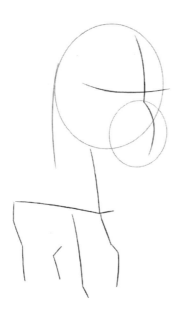

2. Add guidelines to the circles to help place his facial features. Sketch lines for his body and legs. Señor Carrots may be smaller than a horse, but their frameworks are very similar.

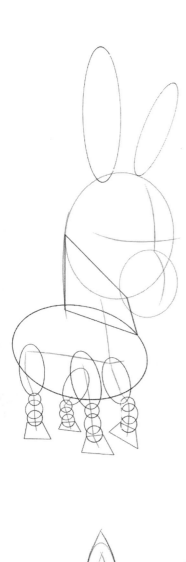

3. Add shape to your drawing. The large oval that outlines his body will overlap with the upper parts of his legs. It is useful to lightly sketch full shapes here to keep your drawing in proportion. Draw trapezoids for his neck and hooves, circles for his lower legs, and two long ovals for his ears.

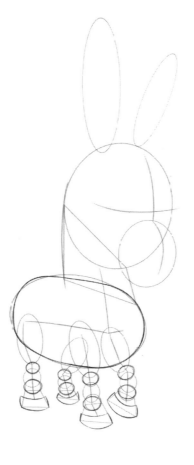

4. Continue adding shape to your drawing, taking care to get his form right. His body isn't perfectly round, so square off your edges to create his sturdy build. Define the shape of his hooves.

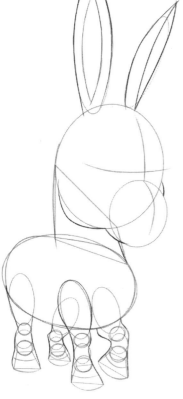

5. Add shape to Señor Carrots's large ears. Outline his jawline, which is rounder and wider than a horse's. Add definition to his legs, carefully following the shape of the circles in your outline sketch.

6. Sketch Señor Carrots's facial features. He has large eyes, and his upper lip sticks out slightly farther than his lower lip, curling into a smile. Draw his mane, with hair falling forward in sections, each coming to a scruffy point. Outline his short, fluffy tail.

7. With a clear outline of Señor Carrots now complete, begin erasing your guidelines and firming up your pencilwork. Start adding detail to his body, outlining tufts of hair around his chest and hooves.

8. Erase any remaining guidelines. Using heavy strokes, shade Señor Carrots's eyebrows, eyelash lines, pupils, and nostrils.

9. Finish by shading your drawing. Keep your strokes neat and even while using light pressure to shade Señor Carrots's entire body. Gradually build darker areas of shadow, leaving his muzzle, the tips of his inner ears, and the fur on his chest and belly bright white.

1. To capture Spirit, start by establishing the lines of action. Draw two circles and a long, bowed line.

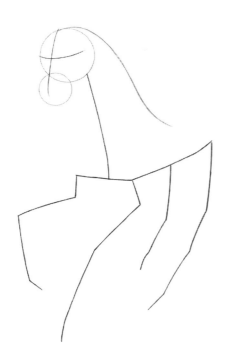

2. Continue building Spirit's framework, penciling in lines for his body and legs. Use foreshortening to make it appear as if Spirit is running toward you. The proportions of your sketch will look a little skewed, with some parts of his body looking larger than others.

76

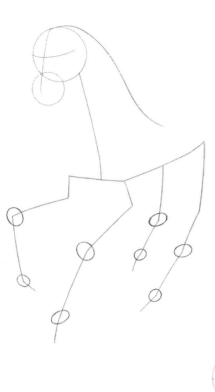

3. Identify the position of Spirit's knees, fetlocks, and hocks. This will help capture the shape of his legs.

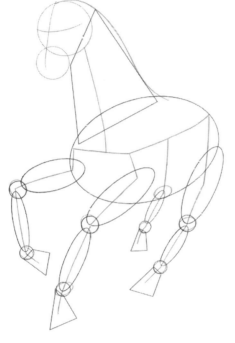

4. Outline Spirit's body, using basic shapes. Use one long oval for his body. Remember, not all the sections in his legs will be the same size, helping create the illusion he is moving forward.

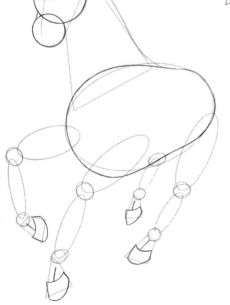

5. Reshape Spirit's body, becoming slimmer toward the back end. Draw his hooves. Each one is slightly different depending on the angle of his foot. Sketch a short line from his ankle joint to the top of the hoof to identify the center point of each hoof, where the curve will be most prominent.

6. Sketch Spirit's facial features, giving him a confident expression. Outline his hair, with his tail extending dynamically behind him as he moves quickly.

7. Highlight the sections in Spirit's mane and tail. Each line should follow the direction of his hair, creating the illusion his mane is being pushed back by the wind and his tail is bouncing with the movement.

8. Erase any remaining guidelines and firmly pencil in your outline. Shade Spirit's eyes, eyebrows, and nostrils. Draw lines to define his chest, shoulders, and neck.

9. Finish by shading your drawing. Move your pencil in the direction the hair falls to create a sense of movement through his mane and tail. You're ready to canter through town.

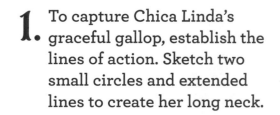

HOW TO DRAW:
CHICA LINDA
IN ACTION

1. To capture Chica Linda's graceful gallop, establish the lines of action. Sketch two small circles and extended lines to create her long neck.

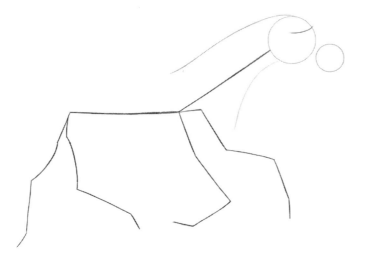

2. Using simple lines, continue building your framework. Consider the positioning of each leg as Chica Linda runs. It can be helpful to look at pictures and videos of horses cantering and galloping to study how their legs move.

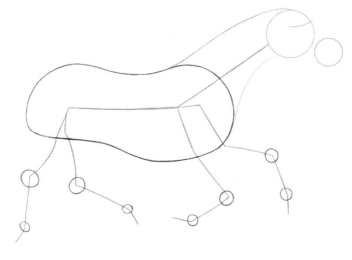

3. Mark the position of Chica Linda's joints with circles. Draw a curved shape for her body. Remember, a horse's body can be broken down into circles if this shape seems complicated.

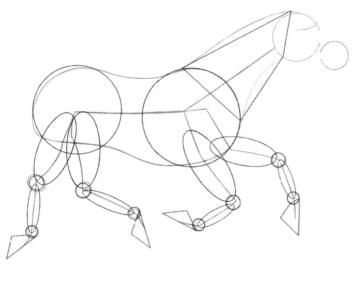

4. Continue adding shape to Chica Linda's body. Use triangles to outline her feet and a large trapezoid for her neck.

5. Use curved lines to add form to her muzzle and jawline. Draw one long line stretching from the base of her jaw, running all the way to her hind legs, following the shape of your guidelines carefully. Begin adding shape to her legs and hooves. We're viewing her from the side, so take care defining her pastern (the indent in her leg above each hoof).

6. Draw her facial features, keeping her expression soft and happy. Her eye should be in line with her nostril. Although she's moving quickly, the hair on her mane and tail still move in neat sections with only a few waves.

7. Start erasing rough pencilwork. You should have a clear outline of Chica Linda. Add short lines to her mane and tail, following the direction of the hair's flow to create a sense of movement.

8. Firm up your outline and erase any remaining guidelines. Shade her eyebrow, pupil, nostril, and eyelash lines, with her eyelashes coming to a neat point at the outer corner of her eye. Sketch a few faint lines to create muscle definition.

9. Add value to your drawing, starting with an even gray base. Ensure your strokes follow the shape of Chica Linda's body to add definition. Shade a dark shadow along her belly and leave white highlights across her back, neck, and head to reflect her shiny coat.

1. To start drawing Boomerang's extended trot, establish the lines of action. Sketch two circles and two curved lines. Leave a small gap between your circles to give his muzzle length.

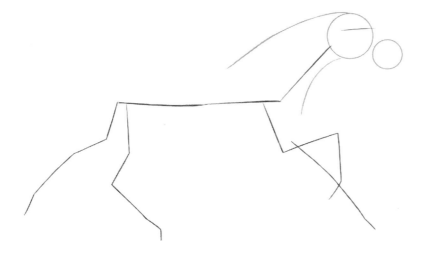

2. Continue drawing his framework. Carefully copy the reference picture when sketching the outline of his legs. Notice the diagonal line for his front left leg doesn't connect to the central part of his frame.

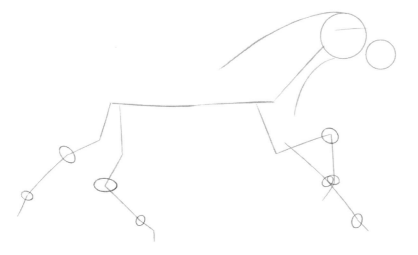

3. Identify the position of Boomerang's joints. He is mid-lope, so his legs are in different positions. Although his rear left leg is extended, notice that it still curves slightly around the joints.

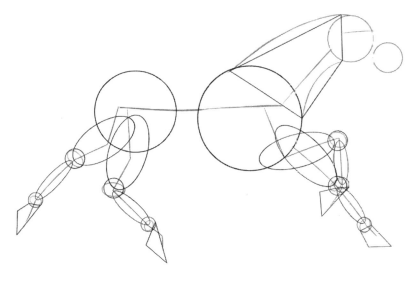

4. It's time to add shape to your framework. Draw two large circles for Boomerang's body and a large trapezoid for his neck. From this angle, his feet look triangular.

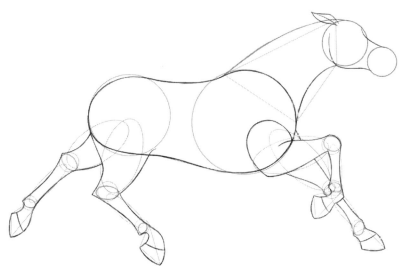

5. Start defining Boomerang's outline, keeping your lines light. Round his jawline and draw an arched line stretching from his forehead to his muzzle. Draw a line around the two large circles. Add form to his legs and hooves, emphasizing the shape of his active limbs. Draw his ear, angled back against the wind.

6. Pencil in Boomerang's facial features. His eye is wide, and he has a happy smile. The curves of his muzzle are more prominent at this angle. Outline his mane and tail, with the hair flowing backward from the momentum of running.

7. Begin erasing rough pencilwork and start adding detail to your drawing. Use soft lines to outline Boomerang's patches. Create a sense of movement in his mane and tail by adding light lines, following the shape of the hair.

8. Firm up your outline and erase any remaining guidelines. Shade his eyebrow, pupil, and nostril. Use a thick black line to define his long eyelashes, following the shape of his eyelid. Draw a line on his neck.

9. Add a touch of shading to your drawing. Keep your strokes short and light when shading his coat, moving your hand in the direction of the hair to give it texture. Follow the curve of your hooves to emphasize their rounded shape.

1. To draw Spirit in a bold stance, establish the lines of action. Sketch two circles and arched lines.

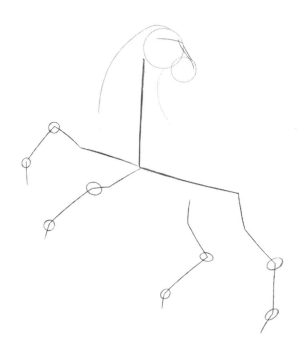

2. Continue building Spirit's framework. To capture the dynamic movement, it is useful to identify where Spirit's joints will lie at this stage, then use simple lines to connect them.

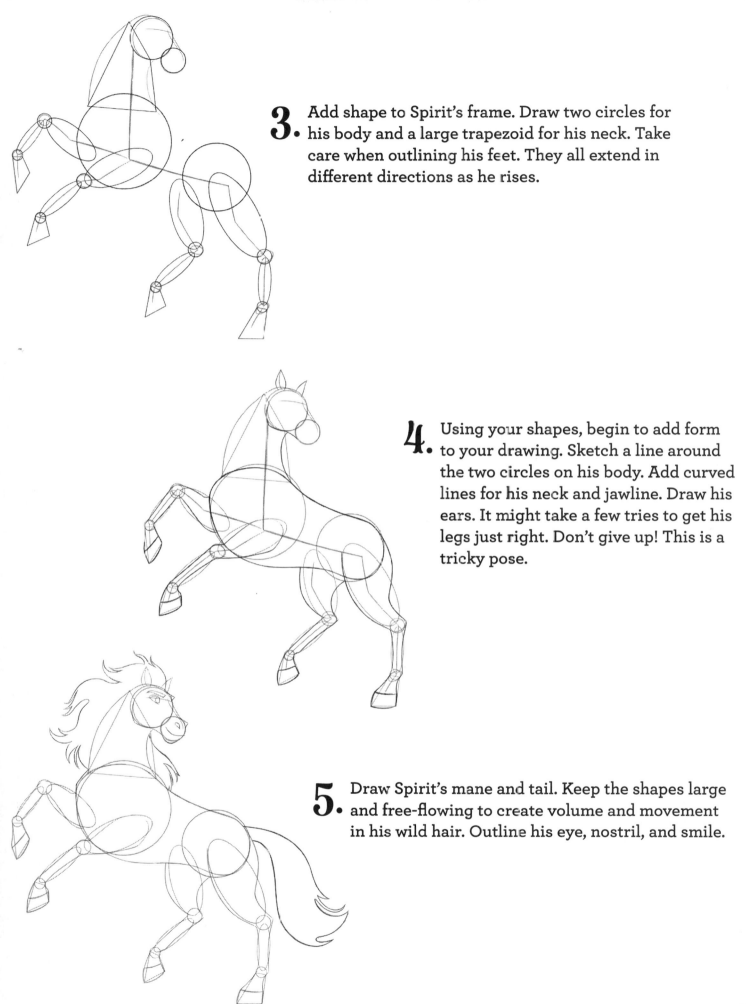

3. Add shape to Spirit's frame. Draw two circles for his body and a large trapezoid for his neck. Take care when outlining his feet. They all extend in different directions as he rises.

4. Using your shapes, begin to add form to your drawing. Sketch a line around the two circles on his body. Add curved lines for his neck and jawline. Draw his ears. It might take a few tries to get his legs just right. Don't give up! This is a tricky pose.

5. Draw Spirit's mane and tail. Keep the shapes large and free-flowing to create volume and movement in his wild hair. Outline his eye, nostril, and smile.

6. Start erasing rough linework. Continue adding shape to Spirit's mane and tail, with the hair falling in sections.

7. Firm up your pencilwork and erase any remaining guidelines. Shade Spirit's pupil, nostril, and eyebrows. Drawing a few short lines can add definition to Spirit's chest and shoulder, as well as highlighting the curve in his neck.

8. Shade your drawing. Although his mane and tail are dark, vary the pressure on your pencil as you make short strokes across the page to add highlights and lowlights, giving the hair texture. Leave white highlights at the front of each hoof to accentuate the curved shape.

HOW TO DRAW:
APPLES

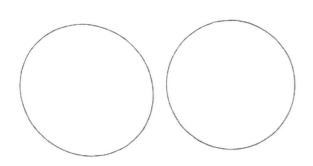

1. Begin by lightly sketching two neat circles.

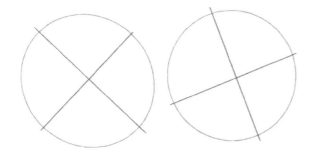

2. Draw guidelines through the center of each circle. The lines should cross in the middle.

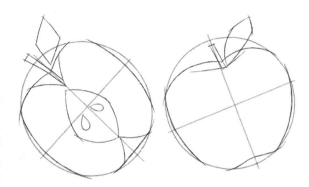

3. Add shape to your apple, including a soft indent at its base. This will be a deeper V shape inside the apple. Draw a thin rectangle for the stalk and a small diamond for the leaf. Sketch an almond shape for the core and two small teardrop shapes for the seeds.

4. Firm up your outlines and erase your guidelines.

5. Shading your apple will make it look good enough to eat! Using circular motions with your pencil, add value to the darkest areas. Leave spots of bright white to give it a delicious shine.

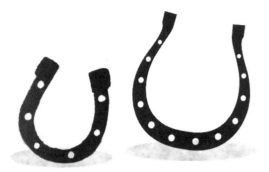

1. Draw two wide rectangles at a slight angle, keeping one slightly smaller than the other.

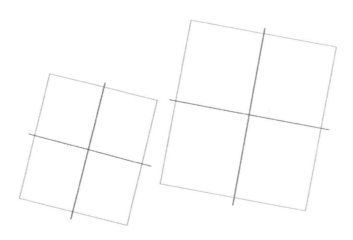

2. Add guidelines to the center of your rectangles. The lines should cross in the middle of the shapes, creating a grid.

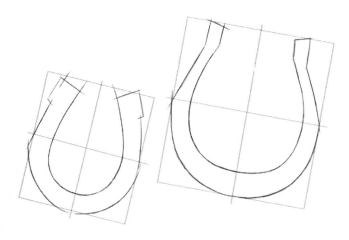

3. Sketch the outline of your horseshoes. Use your grid to break the horseshoe down into smaller sections. They should join to form a large U shape. Play with the form and thickness of each horseshoe's branch and heel.

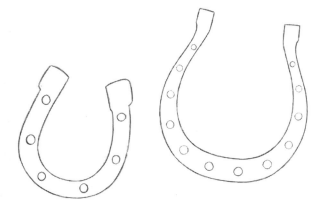

4. Firm up your outline and erase your guidelines. Add a series of small, evenly spaced circles to your horseshoes.

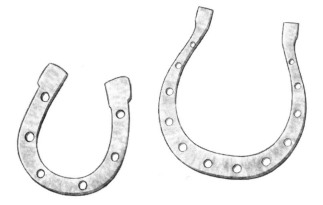

5. Shade your drawing. Leave the nail holes white and add harder lines where shadows fall to create a 3D look.

1. Begin by sketching a rectangle to create a grid for your flower.

2. Add guidelines to your rectangle, splitting it into four equal parts.

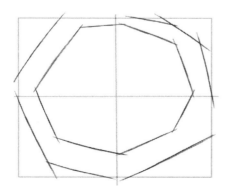

3. Roughly sketch an octagon inside the grid, with a larger heptagon around it. The sides of your shapes do not need to be neat or even—even the prettiest of flowers are not symmetrical!

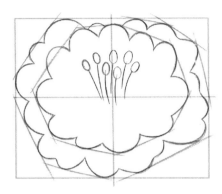

4. Start adding shape to your flower, focusing on one section of your grid at a time. In the center, add a few short lines topped with small egg shapes to form the stamen.

5. Firm up your outlines and erase any rough linework.

6. Finally, shade your drawing. Continue moving your pencil across the page, gradually increasing pressure as you reach the darkest areas to create a smooth transition between tones.

1. Begin by sketching a long, curved framework for your leaf.

2. Add slightly curved lines along each side.

3. Sketch teardrop shapes around your leaf's framework.

4. Firm up your outlines and erase any rough linework.

5. Finally, shade your drawing. Continue moving your pencil across the page, gradually increasing pressure as you reach the darkest areas to create a smooth transition between tones.

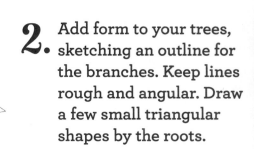

HOW TO DRAW:
TREES

1. Start by sketching a frame for your trees. Have fun playing with short lines jutting in different directions to give their branches an interesting look.

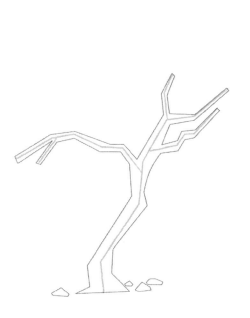

2. Add form to your trees, sketching an outline for the branches. Keep lines rough and angular. Draw a few small triangular shapes by the roots.

3. Use a series of jagged lines to outline the shape of your leaves.

4. Once you're happy with your outlines, begin firming up your pencilwork, adding clear definition to your trunks and branches.

5. Use curved lines to add shape to your leaves and the foliage around the roots.

6. Add detail to your drawing, marking rough lines on the bark of the tree. Use tight, scalloped lines to give your tree a leafy look.

7. Finish by adding value to your drawings. Consider the different textures found on trees. Short, firm lines on the trunk and branches will create a harder look, while light, circular shading will give the leaves a softer look.

HOW TO DRAW:
LUCKY & SPIRIT
CAMEO

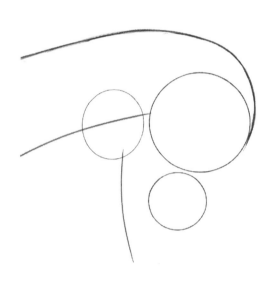

1. Spirit and Lucky really are the best of friends. Begin to capture their kindred spirits by sketching a loose framework, using circles and curved lines.

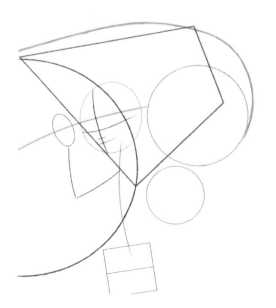

2. Continue building your framework, breaking each part down into simple shapes. A large semicircle creates Spirit's chest, and a trapezoid creates his neck. While lots of these lines will be covered in the final drawing, lightly sketching the full outline will help keep your image in proportion.

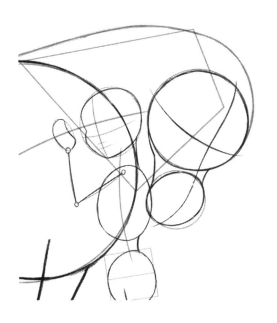

3. Sketch ovals for Lucky's upper body and pelvis. Add definition to the shape of her head and visible hand. Mark faint guidelines for Lucky's and Spirit's facial features. Draw two short lines for Spirit's legs.

4. Start adding shape to Lucky's body, fully outlining her torso and her arm. Sketch Spirit's ears and outline his legs, following your guidelines.

5. Define the shape of Spirit's face, his muzzle gently resting on Lucky's back. Draw his facial features, with his eyes looking kindly down toward her. Sketch the outline of his mane, with a lock falling over the front of his head as he bends forward.

6. Draw Lucky's features. Unlike Spirit, her eyes are wide as she looks up at her friend. Sketch the outline of her hair. Her curls are similar to those in Spirit's wild mane!

7. With your outline complete, firm up your pencilwork. Use bold lines when outlining Spirit. Both sets of eyebrows and eyelash lines should be filled with dark shading. Add shape to Lucky's outfit.

8. Color Lucky's pupils and draw the floral design on her top. Fabric tends to follow a person's figure, and so does any decorative pattern. Notice that the dark lines on Lucky's top follow the curve of her sleeve and shape of her torso.

9. Let's add a decorative frame! Outline your drawing with a large oval shape, with two smaller ovals at either side. You may choose to include the full drawing inside your frame or crop it slightly, as shown here.

10. Inside each of the smaller ovals, draw a series of circles. Keep your lines light.

11. Using your circle guides, draw flowers and leaves. Carefully outline the larger oval with two thin lines, creating a frame.

12. Erase any remaining guidelines, as well as any lines which extend outside of your frame.

13. Finish by shading your drawing, using soft, gentle strokes to perfectly capture their caring friendship! Add light shadows around Spirit's eyes. Create bright highlights in Lucky's hair with your eraser.

Illustrations by Fabio Laguna

Cover design by Paul Banks. Cover illustration by Fabio Laguna.

Little, Brown and Company
Hachette Book Group
1290 Avenue of the Americas, New York, NY 10104
Visit us at LBYR.com

First Edition: July 2021

Little, Brown and Company is a division of Hachette Book Group, Inc. The Little, Brown name and logo are trademarks of Hachette Book Group, Inc.

The publisher is not responsible for websites (or their content) that are not owned by the publisher.

Library of Congress Control Number: 2021934896

ISBNs: 978-0-316-62805-1 (paperback), 978-0-316-62808-2 (ebook), 978-0-316-62809-9 (ebook), 978-0-316-62807-5 (ebook)

PRINTED IN THE UNITED STATES OF AMERICA

CW

10 9 8 7 6 5 4 3 2 1